SOUPS

OF

CHATEAU

DE

VERZAT

A Companion Cookbook to the
Château de Verzat Series

DEBRA BORCHERT

LE
VIN
PRESS

Cover design by Lynn Andreozzi
Book designed and typeset by Bookery

Published by Le Vin Press
Year of Publication: 2023

E-book ISBN: 978-0-9894545-8-2
Trade paperback ISBN: 978-0-9894545-9-9

First Edition

DEDICATED TO ALL MY SOUP PARTY GUESTS

WITHOUT MY REALIZING IT,

YOU WERE MY FIRST TASTE TESTERS.

Merci

CONTENTS

THE STORY
OF SOUP

SOUP MAY HAVE BEEN
THE FIRST FAST FOOD

D URING THE 18ᵀᴴ century in Paris, France, people lived in lodgings, usually one room with, if one was lucky, a fireplace. Unlucky people had no way of cooking. They hauled their water from public fountains for cooking and washing, and they used chamber pots (which they emptied on the streets) for their bathrooms.

BRANDY SELLER by
Anne Claude Philippe de Tubières,
comte de Caylus
The Metropolitan Museum of Art
Curtesy WikiMedia Commons

Parisian markets offered fruits, vegetables, cheeses, breads, fish, chickens, rabbits, and cuts and organs of lamb, pork, and beef. Vendors roved the streets. These sellers carried vessels, which held liquids like vinegar, brandy, wine, hot chocolate, lemonade, coffee, and milk, which they dispensed into wooden or metal cups for consumption. Roving vendors also dispensed clear bullions which were popular "restoratifs," restoratives. According to the *Online Etymology Dictionary,* the word restaurant was initially used to describe a variety of rich, meat-based bouillons.

Prior to the French Revolution (the beginning of which most historians agree was July 14, 1789, with the storming of the Bastille) there were plenty of cafés and bars where one went for gossip, political discussion, and liquid refreshment. But after the social upheaval—when market women marched to Versailles and brought the Royal family to Paris so the King could see first-hand, his starving subjects—nobles fled the country, and many chefs and servants lost their employment.

Those unemployed culinary experts started eating establishments, where hearty soups and stews were served to those who could afford a meal. Soon, one could enjoy a hot dinner and not worry about cooking or cleaning up.

DRINKS VENDOR by
Anne Claude Philippe de Tubières,
comte de Caylus
The Metropolitan Museum of Art
Curtesy WikiMedia Commons

People lucky enough to have a fireplace and eager to feed their starving families, copied the new mouth-watering dishes that only the aristocrats could afford at restaurants. I honor those commoners and vendors who invented tasty, wholesome soups to feed the poor, with this book.

Soups were and are the lifeblood of many Parisians. Even today, people in France wonder why Americans use the term *homemade*—as if there is any other kind of soup. Since soups were a main culinary staple, I developed recipes for my characters.

In many recipes, I've included excerpts from the three volumes belonging to the Château de Verzat Series. These scenes demonstrate the importance of soups in the cuisine and culture of 18th century France.

I hope you enjoy the recipes I've created with the intent of preparing food in healthy and flavorful ways for your loved ones.

Bon Appetit!

RECIPES

AURÉLIA'S ROASTED PUMPKIN SOUP

SERVES 4-6

*When Aurélia arrives in America, she is eager to cook. She is
thrilled to discover foods she ate in her homeland and takes
over the kitchen, much to the delight of Henri and Joliette.*

INGREDIENTS

2 small baking or 1 medium fresh pumpkin*

1 small onion, quartered

extra virgin olive oil

½ cup water

sea salt

freshly ground black pepper

1 ½ quarts chicken or vegetable broth

¼–½ teaspoon ground coriander

¼–½ teaspoon cumin

1 or 2 dashes of ground cloves

1 tablespoon grated fresh ginger

chopped fresh marjoram or parsley (optional)

PROCESS

1. Preheat oven to 425° F.

2. Cut the pumpkin into quarters and remove the seeds and fibrous strands.

3. Place the pieces of pumpkin, skin side down, in a roasting pan and pour a bit of water around them, just enough to prevent the skins from sticking to make cleanup easier.

4. Place the ¼ of an onion in the center of the pumpkin pieces.

5. Spray olive oil over the cut sides of the onions and pumpkin flesh and season with salt and pepper.

6. Roasting time varies depending on the size of the pieces of pumpkin. Roast for 30–60 minutes. Some black edges are fine. The pumpkin is done when it is easy to pierce the pumpkin flesh with a sharp knife.

7. Allow the pumpkin and onions to cool.

8. When cool, scoop out the pumpkin and place the flesh and onions in the bowl of a food processor in batches. Blitz the pumpkin and onions, adding a bit of broth to make a thick purée.

9. Pour the purée into a heavy bottomed pan and add as much of the broth for the thickness of soup you like.

10. Cook the soup on low. When hot, stir in the spices and grated fresh ginger, according to your own taste.

11. Sprinkle fresh herbs on each serving.

NOTES

1. *Canned pumpkin will *not* work for this recipe.

2. This soup freezes well.

DEBRA'S BLACK BEAN, YAM AND TURKEY SAUSAGE CHILI

SERVES 4–6

This is one of My Chevalier's favorite stews. I served this dish for my cast of characters and asked for their honest critique. Louis loved the zing of chili powder. Joliette enjoyed the surprising inclusion of yams. Aurélia said this stew

reminded her of home. Geneviève agreed to make it if she could borrow my slow cooker and some electricity. Simon and Fortuné were glad I included Love Apples (tomatoes). And Henri claimed it was almost as wonderful as his maman's White Bean Soup.

Everyone insisted I include this recipe in the book. I protested, "This is not French cuisine!" They did not care. They demanded I include it, or they would stop speaking to me. I complied.

INGREDIENTS

1–2 tablespoons extra virgin olive oil

½ teaspoon ground chipotle chili* powder (for milder chili, use just a dash)

1 pound turkey sausage, diced into bite-size pieces (optional)

2 cans (15-ounce) black beans, rinsed and drained

2 large yams peeled and diced into half-inch cubes

2 ½ cups beef broth (2, 15-ounce cans are fine)

1 large onion, diced

¼ teaspoon sea salt

4 cloves garlic, minced

1 can (14-ounce) diced tomatoes with chilies

1–2 tablespoons chili powder

freshly squeezed juice of 2 limes

1 tablespoon ground cumin

½ cup chopped fresh cilantro (optional)

PROCESS

1. Heat oil in a heavy-bottomed pan, like a Dutch oven, over medium heat. Brown turkey sausage pieces in batches and remove and drain pieces on paper towel when browned.

2.   After removing browned sausage, add onion (and additional oil if needed) and cook, stirring often, until the onion begins to soften, about 4 minutes.

3.   Add yams, garlic, chili powder, cumin, chipotle chili powder, and salt. Cook, stirring constantly, for a minute.

4.   Add browned sausage pieces and broth and bring to a simmer.

5.   Cover, reduce heat, and simmer until the yams are not quite cooked through, 10–12 minutes.

6.   Add beans and tomatoes and return to a simmer, stirring often for about 15 minutes. Remove from heat and stir in lime juice. Sprinkle cilantro on each serving.

NOTES

1.   You can use cayenne pepper instead of chipotle, but it will be missing the smokey flavor.

2.   Cooking in a Slow Cooker: You can make this recipe in a slow cooker, just brown the sausage first, then add all ingredients, except lime juice and cilantro, in the order in which they are listed. Cook on high for 4–6 hours. If the stew has too much liquid, leave the cover ajar for steam to escape for half an hour of cooking time. Add the lime juice and cilantro right before serving.

3.   As some people dislike cilantro, I serve it on the side.

DEBRA'S ZUCCHINI SOUP

SERVES 4

When our friend Mireille gifted us her Parisian apartment for two weeks as a wedding gift, my fiancé and I did not hesitate to book a flight. Mireille greeted her jet-lagged friends with a delightful soup. After one delicious sip I asked if it was homemade.

"Is there any other kind of soup besides homemade?" she
asked.

*She kindly shared her recipe, which I've Americanized
and added a cold option.*

Merci, Mireille!

INGREDIENTS

2 pounds zucchini

½–1 quart chicken or vegetable broth

extra virgin olive oil

sea salt and white pepper

fresh herbs (basil, parsley, or thyme)

flavored olive oil for drizzling (optional)*

PROCESS

1. Wash zucchini and allow to dry. Do not peel.
2. Quarter the zucchini lengthwise and chop into ¼ inch cubes.
3. Heat a heavy-bottomed pot on low. Add a splash of olive oil and the zucchini.
4. Cook on low, stirring occasionally, until the zucchini is limp.
5. Add enough broth to cover the zucchini and cook until zucchini is cooked through.
6. Allow soup to cool.
7. When the soup is cool, use an immersion blender and process the soup to the thickness you prefer. If you like it less thick, add a bit of broth. If you'd like it to be thicker, continue to simmer until the excess liquid evaporates.

8. Bring the soup to a simmer. When hot, garnish each serving with chopped fresh herbs such as parsley or thyme.

COLD OPTION

1. If serving the soup cold, cook as above steps 1–6, and allow to cool.
2. If you like the soup to have a delicate basil flavor, add fresh basil and process it along with the cooked zucchini.
3. Refrigerate until cold.
4. Add chopped fresh basil to each serving.
5. Add a swirl of flavored olive oil*.

NOTES

1. *My favorite flavored olive oil for this soup is OMG!'s Herbs de Provence.
2. This recipe can easily be doubled, and it freezes well.

ETTY'S ASPARAGUS SOUP

SERVES 4–6

Secretly, Geneviève must earn money for passage to America to join her lover, Henri. Although she is at odds with her stepmother, Etty, Geneviève does love the woman's soups.

INGREDIENTS

2 pounds asparagus

1–1 ½ quarts chicken or vegetable broth

1 large shallot, diced

dash of cayenne pepper

2–4 tablespoons extra virgin olive oil

1 teaspoon chopped fresh marjoram (optional)

sea salt and white pepper

chopped fresh parsley (optional)

PROCESS

1. Preheat oven to 425° F.
2. Break off woody stems of asparagus spears and discard them.
3. Rinse spears. Chop spears into one-inch pieces and allow to dry on towel.
4. Dice the shallot.
5. Sprinkle olive oil on bottom of roasting pan, add asparagus, and shake the pan to distribute the oil.
6. Roast for 20 minutes at 425°, stirring and shaking every five minutes.
7. Add chopped shallot, stir, roast another 10 minutes or until asparagus is cooked through with some browned spots.
8. When spears are fully cooked, remove pan from oven and allow vegetables to cool.
9. Add cool vegetables to food processor and blitz, adding a bit of broth, until smooth. Add as much broth as you prefer for the consistency and texture of soup you like.
10. Place mixture in heavy-bottomed pan, add as much broth as you like and heat on low. (The soup will continue to thicken as it heats.)

11. Add salt and a few grinds of white pepper to taste.
12. Add cayenne pepper and marjoram (if using) to taste.
13. Sprinkle parsley on each serving.

NOTES

1. This recipe may be doubled or tripled for a crowd. It freezes well.
2. This soup can also be served cold. Add a squeeze of lemon for brightness.

HER OWN REVOLUTION

3

I LAUNCHED MY SCHEME at dinner. A pristine white linen cloth covered the table. Two Sèvres porcelain candlesticks flanked the matching tureen, sitting at the table's center. A violent decoration for a dining room, with two red foxes climbing the taper holders and hunting exotic birds around the bowl of the tureen.

My stepmother sat, like a hen on a nest, next to my father. Her gold-colored gown cast a waxy yellow hue to her skin, accenting the wrinkles that crisscrossed her neck and bulging bosom. At her shoulder, an ornate brooch sparked in the candlelight.

Forcing myself to speak before my throat closed, I rushed my words. "Papa, I learned much about laws while I clerked for you last year." I did not say I needed to understand the idiotic laws if I was going to violate them. I sipped my wine. "Now that the Committee of Public Safety is in control, and the sans-culottes have not rioted in months, I wish to resume my duties to learn of our new government."

My stepmother clinked her spoon against her bowl. "My dear, it is dangerous for a woman to leave her home. You worry your dear papa. Antoine, you should never have allowed her to clerk." She pat, pat, patted Papa's elbow, making him smile.

I nodded like I agreed—but I wanted to shout, women deserve the right to have an education and jobs other than doing laundry or selling fish. Just as Henri had spoken at the National Assembly. If there were such a law, I would not have had to impersonate my brother to attend University, and I could become an attorney, like Henri.

Papa inhaled the steam rising from his asparagus soup, looked up, and blinked. His curving hairline and whiskers made his face a heart shape, and his narrow nose and round eyes gave him the appearance of a confused, loveable bird. I wanted to hug him.

ETTY'S CARROT-GINGER SOUP

SERVES 4–6

Featured in *A Taste of France*

Geneviève is desperate for her father's help, and so she dresses with the intent of convincing him to release her friend from prison.

INGREDIENTS

1 pound baby carrots

1 sweet onion, diced

¼ cup extra virgin olive oil

juice and zest of one orange

1–1 ½ quarts chicken or vegetable broth

fresh ginger, grated

dash cayenne pepper

sea salt

white pepper

chopped fresh parsley or marjoram

PROCESS

1. Preheat oven to 425° F.
2. Wash and peel carrots and allow to dry on a towel.
3. Sprinkle olive oil on bottom of roasting pan, add carrots, season with salt and pepper to taste, toss to coat carrots, and stir.
4. Roast for 20 minutes, stirring carrots every five minutes. Add diced onion, stir, roast another 10–20 minutes, or until carrots are cooked through with some blackened spots.
5. When carrots are fully cooked, remove pan from oven and allow to cool.
6. Add cool vegetables to food processor and blitz adding a bit of broth, until smooth.
7. Place mixture in heavy-bottomed pan, add enough broth for the consistency and texture of soup you like.

8. Heat soup on low. (The soup will continue to thicken as it heats.)
9. Add orange juice, orange zest, grated ginger, and cayenne pepper to taste.
10. Sprinkle parsley or marjoram on top of each serving.

NOTES

1. This recipe may be doubled or tripled for a crowd. It freezes well.

HER OWN REVOLUTION

II

THE AROMA OF carrot-ginger soup heartened me. It was Papa's favorite potage, and I hoped it would help make him grant my request. I wove Maman's yellow ribbon through my hair, pinched my cheeks, and quietly entered the dining room. "Good evening."

"Good evening, my dear. We've already begun. Sit down." Etty placed her hand protectively atop her precious tureen and put out her hand for my bowl. She was on her best behavior in Papa's presence. The smile I gave her sealed our pact. She'd keep Henri's letter a secret as long as I had her brooch.

FORTUNÉ AND SIMON'S ROASTED TOMATO SOUP WITH GARLIC CROUTONS

SERVES 4–6

Henri promised Bertrand to care for his wife and son, Simon, should anything happen to him. Henri took Simon under his wing and acted as his older brother. When Fortuné arrived at Château de Verzat, mischievous Simon took cheeky Fortuné under his wing. About this time, France began to accept the tomato, which most Europeans thought to be poisonous. The French called tomatoes, Pomme d'Amour, Love Apples, and tomatoes flourished in the Loire Valley.

Thinking they could make a love potion, Simon and Fortuné created this soup. They also realized it is the perfect accompaniment to something else they adored: bread flavored with garlic.

INGREDIENTS

4 pounds ripe tomatoes

¼ cup extra virgin olive oil

4–6 cloves of garlic

a splash of red wine

1 ½–2 quarts chicken or vegetable broth

1 stale baguette

sea salt and pepper to taste

chopped fresh parsley or oregano (optional)

PROCESS

1. Preheat oven to 425° F.

2. Quarter the tomatoes and cut out and discard the woody stem.

3. Coat the bottom of a large roasting pan with olive oil. You may need two roasting pans depending on the size of the tomatoes. Don't crowd them.

4. Toss the tomatoes in the pan with a bit more olive oil.

5. Remove the papery skins of 3–4 garlic cloves and toss the cloves in with the tomatoes.

6. Sprinkle with salt and pepper.

7. Roast the tomatoes until edges are charred. There should be quite a bit of liquid. If the tomatoes seem dry, lower the temperature to 400 and continue to cook.

8. Remove tomatoes from the oven and allow to cool.

9. In batches, pour the tomatoes and garlic into a food processor and blitz with broth until smooth. As the batches are processed, pour them into a heavy-bottomed pan.

10. Place the empty roasting pan on a low to medium flame. When hot, deglaze the pan with a few splashes of wine. Scrape the fond from the sides of the pan into the tomato juices and wine. Allow to cool.

11. Add the pan juices to the tomato mixture and cook over low heat.

12. Add as much broth as you like for the thickness of soup you prefer and simmer.

13. Cut the stale baguette into cubes.

14. Pour the olive oil into a pan and set the heat to low.

15. Add the remaining garlic cloves and cook for 30 seconds. Do not allow them to brown. Remove and discard the garlic, which has flavored the oil, before adding the bread cubes.

16. Add the bread cubes in batches and cook until they are toasty and lightly browned.

17. Remove the cubes as they are browned and allow them to cool on a rack.

18. When the soup is piping hot, serve with a sprinkle of croutons and herbs.

NOTES

1. This soup freezes well.
2. I sometimes drizzle a bit of OMG! Sundried Tomato Balsamic Dipping Oil over each serving. (See Resources.)

GENEVIÈVE'S EASY LEMON CHICKEN ORZO SOUP

SERVES 4–6

Geneviève does not cook. Ever resourceful, when she's forced to cook, she makes use of Madame Detré's Fabulous Roasted Chicken—if there is any left. As I do not have that luxury, I use leftover rotisserie chicken.

INGREDIENTS

2 quarts chicken broth

2–3 cups chopped rotisserie chicken

juice of 2 lemons

¼ cup white wine

1 cup orzo pasta

4 cups fresh spinach (optional)

chopped fresh mint or parsley

freshly ground white pepper to taste

PROCESS

1. Heat chicken broth over low flame until simmering.
2. Add chicken, lemon juice, and wine.
3. Return to simmer, stirring occasionally.
4. Add orzo and stir often for eight minutes.
5. Add spinach, if using, cover and allow spinach to wilt.
6. The soup will thicken, so taste frequently to check doneness of pasta.
7. When orzo is al dente, remove from heat and serve immediately.
8. Add pepper to taste and chopped herbs atop each serving.

NOTES

1. Leftover soup will thicken due to the starch in the pasta. Add more chicken broth if you like your soup less thick.
2. Substitute rice or barley for the orzo if serving in a slow cooker as the pasta will continue to cook and the soup will thicken too much.

EXCERPT FROM:

HER OWN War

43

A BOWL OF LEMONS stood at the corner of the chopping block, reminding me of the invisible letter Tante Nicole had written to me. Tante had tended the lemon trees in the glass-covered terrace like a maman tended a newborn. She had said she liked lemon with her tisane, yet I'd never seen her put lemon in any drink. I cut and squeezed a lemon into a bowl and took the juice and the book to the table and lit another candle.

I stared at the notes I'd written. This was where Tante Nicole's work had left off. If I continued it, and was caught, I could be executed as a traitor. And Revolutionaries could execute everyone on the estate...

HARVEST VEGETABLE AND FRUIT SOUP

SERVES 6–8

*This soup is made like stone soup—by the entire community.
During the vendanges, the grape harvest, all the people
who are not picking, pitch in and make a soup of vegetables
and fruits that are ripening in the gardens on the estate.*

Depending on the garden varieties at Château de Verzat,
the recipe varies, and so this recipe contains suggestions
for a harvest soup designed around whatever is in season.

INGREDIENTS

1 butternut squash, peeled and diced in 1-inch cubes

1 Comice or Bartlett pear, cored and cut into 1-inch cubes (don't peel)

2 parsnips, peeled and cut into 1-inch cubes

1 ½–2 quarts chicken or vegetable broth

2 carrots, peeled and cut into 1-inch cubes

sea salt and freshly ground white pepper

2 leeks, cleaned and white parts sliced

5 sprigs of fresh thyme

1 large onion, peeled and diced

dash cayenne pepper (optional)

extra virgin olive oil

lemon wedges

1 Granny Smith apple, cored and cut into 1-inch cubes (don't peel)

chopped fresh parsley

PROCESS

1. Preheat oven to 425° F.
2. Coat the bottom of a heavy roasting pan with olive oil.
3. Add the chunks of squash, parsnips, and carrots and roast for 10 minutes.
4. Add the onions and leeks and stir. Continue roasting for another 10 minutes, shaking pan frequently.
5. Add the apple and pear chunks and roast for about 10–15 minutes until all the vegetables and fruits are soft. Blackened

edges are fine, but don't allow the fruits to burn.

6. Remove pan from oven and allow vegetables and fruits to cool.

7. Working in batches, pour vegetables and fruits with a few splashes of broth in the bowl of a food processor and blitz until the mixture is smooth, yet a bit chunky.

8. When the mixture is finished puréeing, pour into a heavy-bottomed pot.

9. Add the remaining broth to the puréed mixture and heat on low, stirring frequently.

10. When hot, add salt and pepper to taste, the thyme leaves, and a dash of cayenne pepper, if using. Feel free to add a squirt of lemon juice for brightness.

11. Heat through and serve with a sprinkling of chopped parsley and a lemon wedge.

NOTES

1. This soup freezes well.

2. Feel free to experiment, using other vegetables like cabbage, potatoes, turnips, yams, and other squashes.

HENRI'S FAVORITE, CHILLED SWEET AND SPICY CORN SOUP

SERVES 4–6

*When Henri arrived in America, he accompanied Aurélia
to the market where she plucked up six ears of corn and lov-*

ingly placed them in her basket. He couldn't tell her that, in France, corn was not eaten by people but fed to animals.

When they returned, Aurélia shucked the husks and cut the corn from the cobs. The scent of the delicate fresh sweetness made Henri's mouth water. When she proudly served him a soup from her homeland, he had to eat it. It was surprisingly delicious. Although this is Aurélia's recipe, incorporating African spices, I've named it after Henri's great appreciation for it.

INGREDIENTS

1 medium Yukon Gold potato, finely chopped

½–2 teaspoons ground coriander

½ red pepper, finely chopped

½–2 teaspoons ground cumin

½ yellow pepper, finely chopped

1 or 2 pinches of ground cloves

½ medium sweet white onion, finely chopped

4 cups of fresh corn kernels (about 5 ears)

1 quart water

extra virgin olive oil

½–1 teaspoon grated Jalapeño pepper*

sea salt and freshly ground white pepper

2 cloves of garlic, minced

juice of 1 lime, and lime wedges

1 tablespoon grated fresh ginger

chopped fresh cilantro or parsley (optional)

PROCESS

1. Dice all vegetables. (Don't peel the potato if you like the extra texture.)
2. Heat a heavy bottomed soup pot on low and when hot, coat the bottom of the pan lightly with olive oil.
3. Add the potatoes, stirring so they do not stick or brown, and cook for 1 minute.
4. Add the red and yellow pepper and continue to stir for a few minutes until the vegetables soften.
5. Add the onion and garlic with a sprinkle of salt and stir until the onion pieces become translucent. Do not allow to brown.
6. Add the corn and stirring gently, allow the oil to coat the kernels.
7. Add the ginger, coriander, cumin, and cloves to your taste. Stir until incorporated.
8. Add water and heat to a simmer. Once hot, simmer for 20–30 minutes until all vegetables are cooked.
9. Taste the soup and add salt and pepper to your liking.
10. Remove soup from heat and allow it to cool.
11. Using either a food processor or immersion blender, blitz the soup until it is as smooth as you like it. You may need to add a bit more water if you like your soup less thick.
12. Using a grater, finely grate as much of the Jalapeño pepper for as much heat as you like. Stir in lime juice and refrigerate until serving.
13. Serve with chopped fresh herbs and lime wedges on the side.

NOTES

1. *Chopping the Jalapeño pepper will result in chunks that will overwhelm the delicate flavors of this complex soup, so I recommend using a grater.
2. The amount of spices are determined by your tastes. Start out mild; you can always add more for a spicier soup.
3. This soup freezes well.

JOLIETTE'S CHILLED FRESH PEA SOUP

SERVES 6–8

Photo by Debra Borchert

While living in France, Joliette never cooked—she was far too busy fermenting wine. But when she and Henri arrived in America, she longed for dishes made by her beloved Cook.

Joliette remembered afternoons, sitting at Cook's battered wooden table, shelling peas for Cook's sweet and velvety Chilled Fresh Pea Soup. This recipe is based on Joliette's memories and my experimentations.

INGREDIENTS

2 cups fresh or frozen peas

1 cup water

a few sprigs of fresh mint

sea salt (optional)

fruity white balsamic vinegar (optional)*

PROCESS

1. Simmer peas in water until peas are tender.
2. Keeping the broth, drain peas and allow to cool.
3. Using an immersion blender, blitz the peas with enough of the cooking liquid for a consistency and thickness you like.
4. Add salt to taste. Chill.
5. Serve with a mint spear and a drizzle of a fruity white balsamic vinegar.

NOTES

1. *My favorite fruity white balsamic vinegar is OMG!'s D'Anjou Pear White Balsamic Vinegar. See Resources page.
2. This soup freezes well.

JOLIETTE'S CHILLED WHITE GRAPE GAZPACHO

SERVES 4–6

Joliette is forever looking for new ways to incorporate grapes into dishes. Muscadet grapes will give this gazpacho a delicately perfumed and honeyed flavor. Sometimes, she might slip in some gooseberries, but only if they are sweet.

INGREDIENTS

1 cup seedless white grapes

¼ honeydew melon

2 white peaches

1 white nectarine

2 Persian cucumbers, with/without peels

sea salt to taste

juice of 1 or 2 limes or lemons

1–2 tablespoons extra virgin olive oil*

1 tablespoon fruity white balsamic vinegar*

1–2 teaspoons grated small Jalapeño pepper**

fresh mint (optional)

PROCESS

1. Dice all fruits and cucumber to a uniform size. The smaller the dice the more variety of flavors and colors will be in every spoonful. Capture all the juice of the fruit and add to a large bowl. A food processor can be used but be careful not to blitz the fruits into a purée.

2. Gently stir with lime or lemon juice. You may have to increase the amount according to the amount of fruit you use.

3. Add the olive oil and a swirl of white balsamic vinegar and stir.

4. Use a grater to sprinkle a whisper or two of the Jalapeño pepper over the soup and stir.

5. Allow mixture to sit at room temperature for an hour for the flavors to meld.

6. Add a dash of sea salt to taste.

7. Chop some fresh mint and add to gazpacho or add a sprig to every serving.

NOTES:

1. Use whatever quantities you desire for your unique gazpacho. The riper the fruit, the more flavorful your soup will be. If you prefer to use a food processor or blender, the soup will be smooth, thick and a pale green color. If you like a creamier gazpacho, you can add nonfat Greek yogurt and process all the ingredients together.

2. The gazpacho can be refrigerated but allow the soup to come to room temperature before serving.

3. *I cannot cook or toss a salad without the wonderful olive oils and vinegars of a Seattle-based company, OMG! You can find a link to Extra Virgin Olive Oil with Meyer Lemon and Blueberry White Balsamic Vinegar, both of which I use in this recipe, in the Resources section.

4. **Grating the Jalapeño pepper allows for distribution of a delicate heat throughout the soup, without the risk of biting into a chunk of pepper that may dull the tastebuds to the delicate flavors of the gazpacho.

MADAME BOURRAN'S APPLE–PARSNIP SOUP

SERVES 4–6

*Many people died of starvation during the French Revo-
lution due to a few things besides extraordinary weather.
Thousands of servants lost their jobs due to the emigration*

and guillotining of nobles who had employed them. Rev-
olutionaries burned crops. People learned to cook whatever
was available. At the Château de Verzat, Geneviève, and
the group of orphans she's rescued, taste a new soup.

INGREDIENTS

2 pounds parsnips, peeled and diced	sea salt
2 large Granny Smith apples, cored and diced*	pepper
1 small onion, diced	dash of nutmeg
1–2 tablespoons extra virgin olive oil	dash of cayenne pepper
1 ½–2 quarts chicken or vegetable broth	chopped fresh parsley or marjoram

PROCESS

In a large stock pot and over low to medium heat:

1. Sauté parsnips in olive oil for about 5 minutes, do not brown.
2. Add apples and onion, do not brown.
3. Sauté until parsnips, apples, and onions are soft.
4. Add half the broth and cook on low for about 10–15 minutes.
5. Allow mixture to cool.
6. Add cooled mixture to food processor and blitz, adding a bit of broth, until smooth.

7. Return mixture to pot and add enough broth for the consistency of soup that you like and heat on low. (The soup will continue to thicken as it heats.)
8. Add nutmeg, cayenne pepper, salt, and pepper to taste.
9. Sprinkle parsley or marjoram atop each serving.

NOTES

1. *I don't peel the apples as the skin gives the soup more texture, but for a more delicate soup, peel them.
2. This recipe may be doubled or tripled for a crowd. It freezes well.

HER OWN REVOLUTION

19

THE CHÂTEAU'S KITCHEN was bigger than a church and warmer too, with two huge fireplaces, each of them bigger than the cellar the four former Sisters and children had been living in. All the children, the wet nurse, and Sisters sat on benches at a long battered wooden table in the center of the cavernous stone-walled room.

Sister Magali tied the children's serviettes below their chins. The children, wide-eyed, whispered their surprise and delight at the warmth, which came not so much from the fires but from the people gathered at the table. Although not related by blood, they were all family.

"Would you like to hold Louisa?" Madame Detré handed Magdeleine's daughter to me.

My arms were aching for her. I wiped my hands on my breeches and snuggled her to my chest, listening to the contented slurping of the children as they devoured their soup.

A boy's dark eyes followed Madame Bourran as she ladled more apple-parsnip soup for everyone. He lifted his bowl and said, "S'il-vousplaîtmerci," as one word.

"What fine manners you have." Madame ran her knuckle along his cheek.

His smile revealed two missing front teeth. She filled his bowl, and he brought it to his mouth and drank until it was empty. He pulled her sleeve as she finished serving the next child and offered his bowl again.

She laughed and refilled it, seeming to enjoy her role as adopted grand-mère to the children as much as they enjoyed her. She turned to the sideboard and placed more bread in a basket. The boy jumped up, picked up the basket, and offered it to each of the Sisters and then each child.

MADAME DETRÉ'S CHICKEN VEGETABLE SOUP

SERVES 6–8

On the rare occasions Henri's maman had chicken, she would have used the carcass to create a hearty broth. She

shows Henri her love with food in this excerpt.

INGREDIENTS

2 boneless chicken breasts

4 boneless chicken thighs

2 quarts water

3 sprigs rosemary

2 cloves of garlic, peeled, and chopped

extra virgin olive oil

2 carrots, peeled and sliced

2 celery stalks, thinly sliced

1 medium onion, peeled, chopped

1 ½–2 quarts chicken or vegetable broth

dash cayenne pepper (optional)

sea salt

freshly ground pepper

1 cup broccoli florets

chopped fresh parsley

lemon wedges

PROCESS

1. Place chicken, rosemary, and garlic in heavy-bottomed pot and cover with water.
2. Heat on low and allow to simmer, uncovered, until the chicken is tender, about 45 minutes.
3. Remove chicken pieces and allow to cool. Discard rosemary and garlic.
4. OPTIONAL: You can continue to simmer the broth until it is reduced by half and use it as part of the chicken soup, but you'll need to cool and skim it before adding it to the soup. I usually allow it to simmer, cool, skim, and then freeze it

for future use.

5. Heat a heavy-bottomed pot on medium heat and coat the bottom with olive oil.

6. Sauté the carrots, celery, and onion in that order, cooking each for 2–3 minutes before adding the next vegetable.

7. Add chicken pieces. Pour in the broth and simmer for 30–45 minutes.

8. Add dash of cayenne if using. (A dash of cayenne boosts flavor without salt.)

9. Season to taste.

10. Add the broccoli 5 minutes before serving so it remains bright green.* Serve with lemon wedges.

NOTES

1. *When serving this in a slow cooker, I replace the broccoli with green beans which retain their color longer than the broccoli.

2. This soup freezes well but add the broccoli or green beans just before serving.

HER OWN
Legacy
8

MAMAN LADLED SOME liquid into a wooden bowl. "Have some soup."

"I have to deliver the laundry."

"First, eat."

I sat, breathing in the aroma of garlic, onions, chicken. "Maman, can you give me some of the rosemary soap you make?"

Her smile lit up the room like a flaming torch. "I'll give you some for your tutor, also."

I'd bring her some meat and bread. I'd buy her a lace-trimmed handkerchief. I'd show her she was the only maman I ever wanted and would ever need. I'd convince her she'd never lose me. I'd try to tell her I loved her.

MADAME DETRÉ'S WHITE BEAN SOUP

SERVES 4–6

*I asked Henri's maman, Madame Detré, to name the secret
ingredient in her soup that made Henri long for home. She
hid her smile behind her hand and blushed like a schoolgirl.
"Thyme," she replied. As she loves Henri fiercely, I won-
dered if she said, "time."*

INGREDIENTS

1–2 cups cubed ham (optional)

1 onion, chopped

2 cloves garlic, minced

2 carrots, chopped

3 stalks of celery, chopped

extra virgin olive oil

2 (15-ounce) cans white beans (cannellini or navy), rinsed and drained

1–1 ½ quarts chicken or vegetable broth

splash of dry white wine (optional)

pinch of cayenne pepper

sea salt

pepper

bunch of fresh thyme, rinsed and allowed to dry

4 cups fresh kale or spinach, chopped (optional)

PROCESS

1. In a heavy-bottomed large pot, sauté ham in a splash of olive oil.

2. When ham is browned, remove and drain on paper towels.

3. Add more olive oil to pan and sauté onions and garlic with a bit of salt until translucent.

4. Add carrots and celery and stir until lightly coated with oil and cook for about 5 minutes.

5. Put half the beans in a blender with 1 cup of the broth and blend until smooth.

6. Add blended beans and broth, the remainder of the broth, and a splash of wine to the vegetables.

7. Add ham and remaining beans to vegetables and stir.

8. Add cayenne pepper, sea salt, and white pepper to taste.

9. Strip thyme leaves from stalks and add to soup.

10. Cook on low for about 30 minutes, stirring occasionally.

11. Add chopped kale or spinach and stir. Add more broth or a bit of white wine if soup is too thick.

12. Simmer until kale or spinach is cooked through and a bright green.

NOTES

1. This recipe can be easily doubled and freezes well.

2. Vegetarian option: use vegetable broth and omit the ham.

MADAME FRANÇOISE'S FRENCH ONION SOUP

SERVES 4–6

Henri's neighbor, Bertrand is determined to "Fight for a new France" at the Bastille. Henri tries to convince him not to go, for Bertrand could be killed. They argue.

INGREDIENTS

6 large onions, a mix of yellow and red

2 large sweet white onions (such as Vedalia or Walla Walla)

extra virgin olive oil

sea salt and pepper

1–1 ½ quart beef or vegetable broth

2 tablespoons brandy (optional)

1–2 tablespoons of flour (whole wheat pastry flour is heartier than white, but both work)

a few sprigs of fresh thyme

½ a baguette, thinly sliced

1 cup of shredded Gruyere cheese

PROCESS

1. Peel and quarter the onions.
2. Thinly slice the onions. I use a thin blade for my food processor.
3. Heat a large, heavy-bottomed pan on medium to low heat. When hot, coat the bottom with olive oil.
4. Keep the heat setting at medium and add the onions in batches, stirring frequently.
5. Add a sprinkling of salt and cook the onions until limp, about 30–45 minutes.
6. Increase the heat a bit, and cook the onions uncovered for about 45–60 minutes until they turn brown but NOT crispy. (Traditional French onion soup recipes call for the addition of two teaspoons of sugar to aide in the browning. I do not use sugar as I use sweet onions and the red onions also add additional color.)
7. Sprinkle the flour over the onions and stir to completely incorporate.

8. Add enough broth to cover the onions. Add the brandy.
9. Cover and allow to simmer until the broth darkens in color and the onions are thoroughly cooked, about 60 minutes.
10. Sprinkle in thyme leaves, stir, and keep warm.
11. The soup can be served or refrigerated and reheated.
12. Toast the baguette slices.
13. Sprinkle the cheese over the slices and toast until cheese is melted and bubbly. (Place under a broiler if you'd like the cheese browned.)
14. Serve the soup with a slice of the cheesy bread floating atop each serving.

NOTES

1. This recipe can easily be doubled, and the soup freezes well.
2. When serving this at a Soup Party, I keep the soup hot in a slow cooker and place a heated serving tray alongside it. I place the baguette toasts on the tray to keep them warm.

HER OWN
*L*EGACY

32

B ERTRAND SAT ON the edge of the fountain. "Should something happen to me…"

Ash from the fire had landed in the water I'd sipped and sat like grit in my mouth. I spat. How could I get him to see reason?

He wiped his brow. "Continue teaching Simon to read? Look after him?"

My arms hung heavy, limp, useless. Simon would be all alone, like I'd been before Papa arrived, but I'd had Bertrand. "Simon doesn't learn as fast as you." My voice was weak.

He stood and walked away.

"Wait!" I ran after him and shoved coins at him. "Please feed Simon and Madame Françoise. I don't care if you think me a Royalist."

He put his hand around mine. "It would only delay starvation."

"What'll Simon do without you?" I stomped. "What'll *I* do without you?"

He put his hand on my shoulder. "You're an honorable man, Henri—with or without a papa."

He strode away, his broad shoulders straight, his head held high. I wanted to cry out, Don't go! But Bertrand had to be his own man and make his own way, without my help. I shoved my hand into my pouch and rubbed the bear he'd helped me carve, felt the space where its ear should've been. I'd give the money to Madame Françoise. She'd accept it and not tell him.

I walked to their home and knocked.

Madame Françoise opened her door. "Come in. Have you seen Bertrand?"

I held out the *écux*. "He told me to give this to you."

"But where is he?"

I shrugged. "I think he's selling his wooden animals at the Palais-Royal."

She pressed the coins to her heart. "It's enough for porridge and many, many soups. Thank you. Would you like some?"

She was like Maman, insisting I eat my bread.

MY CHEVALIER'S EASY MULLIGATAWNY SOUP

SERVES 6–8

When I began our tradition of annual Souper Soup parties,
I asked My Chevalier if he'd make one. He is not a cook,
but he said he had a recipe from long ago that he'd make if

I helped him. The yellowed, torn recipe had appeared in the October 1972 issue of "Redbook Magazine." I did wonder why a young man would be reading a ladies' magazine but, My Chevalier is a Renaissance man, and that explained it. Berry had written next to it, "Good, but work!" He was right. It seemed to be a two-day process. This is my recipe based on the original.

INGREDIENTS

2 boneless chicken breasts

4 boneless chicken thighs

2 quarts water

1 medium onion, peeled, and finely chopped

1 carrot, peeled and sliced

1 4-ounce can mushroom pieces, drained

1 teaspoon sea salt

¼ cup butter

a dash of cayenne pepper

1 tablespoon turmeric

2 tablespoons ground coriander

¼ teaspoon ground ginger

2 tablespoons black poppy seeds

¼ teaspoon ground cinnamon

1 teaspoon ground cumin

½ cup dried and flaked unsweetened coconut

3 cloves garlic, peeled, and minced

1 cup all-purpose flour

2 cans (15.5-ounce) of garbanzo beans

2 quarts chicken broth

1 tablespoon fresh lemon juice

chopped fresh Italian parsley

PROCESS

1. Place chicken in heavy-bottomed pot and cover with water.

2. Add the diced onion, carrot, drained mushroom pieces, and salt.

3. Heat on low and allow to simmer, uncovered, until the chicken is tender, about 45 minutes.

4. Remove chicken pieces and allow to cool.

5. OPTIONAL: You can continue to simmer the broth until it is reduced by half and use it as part of the chicken broth, but you'll need to cool and skim it before adding it to the soup. I usually allow it to simmer, cool, and then freeze it for future use.

6. Melt the butter in a heavy-bottomed pot over medium heat.

7. When butter is melted, add the spices, coconut, and garlic, stirring constantly.

8. Remove the pan from the heat and add the flour, stirring constantly.

9. Pour beans and a bit of liquid into a food processor or blender and blitz until beans are puréed. Depending on the size of your processor or blender you may need to do this in batches.

10. Return pot to medium heat and add the bean purée and any leftover liquid.

11. Gradually add the chicken broth, stirring constantly, and bring to a boil.

12. Lower heat, cover, and simmer for 15 minutes, stirring frequently.

13. Shred the cool chicken into bite-size pieces.

14. Add the chicken and lemon juice and allow to heat through.

15. Add chopped parsley to each serving.

NOTES

1. This soup freezes well.
2. Because we serve this at our Souper Soup parties, we aim for simplicity and do not add cooked rice. Traditionally, this soup is served over a spoonful of hot rice.

SISTER MAGALI'S VELVETY BUTTERNUT SQUASH AND PEAR SOUP

SERVES 4

During the French Revolution members of the clergy were
forced to take an oath swearing loyalty to their country and

the law, first, before God. Revolutionaries blamed their poverty, in part, on the clergy, as the church paid no taxes prior to the Revolution. As there was no proof one had taken the oath, clergy members were often slaughtered by enraged Revolutionaries.

Many nuns and priests went into hiding. Sister Magali hid the orphans in her charge and convinced Geneviève to help them escape Paris. Although Sister Magali gives up her title and habit, she and the orphans blossom at Château de Verzat. Magali experiments in the kitchen, and because there are plenty of Comice pears grown on the estate, she adds them for a slight sweetness to the delight of the children. This recipe is her creation.

INGREDIENTS

1 large butternut squash	salt
1 Comice or other juicy pear	pepper
1–2 tablespoons extra virgin olive oil	splash of white wine (optional)
1 quart vegetable or chicken broth	fresh marjoram or Italian parsley, chopped

PROCESS

1. Preheat oven to 425° F.
2. Wash and dry the squash and cut in half, lengthwise. Scoop out and discard the seeds.

3. Place the squash halves on a baking sheet, flesh-side up, and spray the flesh with olive oil. Sprinkle salt and pepper on the flesh.

4. Bake squash for about 30–45minutes.

5. Core the pear and chop it into 1-inch cubes.

6. When the squash is done, remove it to a cutting board and allow it to cool.

7. Place the diced pear onto the now empty baking sheet and bake for 15 minutes. The pear may char a bit, which is fine.

8. Allow the squash and pear to cool for at least an hour.

9. When the squash is cool, scoop out the flesh from the shell and place it in the bowl of a food processor. Add the roasted pear.

10. Purée the squash and pear, adding splashes of the broth until the mixture is smooth and a thick consistency.

11. Place the purée in a large pot and add enough broth to make the soup as thick as you like.

12. Simmer over low flame. Add a splash of white wine if you like.

13. When soup is hot, add a dash of cayenne pepper and stir well. Serve hot with a sprinkling of fresh herbs.

NOTES

1. Magali tells me this is an easy soup to make for a crowd. She uses one pear for every butternut squash.

2. Roasting vegetables, before adding them to the soup pot, is a great way to intensify their natural flavors.

3. Puréeing the roasted vegetables makes thick soups, without

adding dairy. There may be some blackened bits after roasting, and that is fine, as the blackened bits will add sweetness to the soup.

4. Adding a dash of cayenne pepper enhances flavors without adding salt.

5. This soup freezes well.

THE VERZAT COOK'S POTATO-LEEK SOUP

SERVES 4

Antoine Parmentier introduced the potato to France. King Louis XVI, wanting to persuade his subjects to eat what they thought were poisonous vegetables, had potatoes served

at a ball where his wife, Queen Marie Antoinette, wore
potato blossoms in her wig. To feed hungry Parisians, pota-
toes were grown in public gardens.

Henri finally met his half-sister under stressful circum-
stances. Having lived in poverty most of his life, he is now
at the Verzat mansion in Paris, and the poor man is a fish
out of water.

INGREDIENTS

2 large leeks

1 pound baby Dutch (or yellow) potatoes

extra virgin olive oil

sea salt & white pepper

1–2 ounces dry white wine

1–1 ½ quarts chicken or vegetable broth

dash cayenne pepper (optional)

chopped fresh parsley

PROCESS

1. Thoroughly clean leeks, chop the white parts, and allow to dry on towel.
2. Dice potatoes (do not peel skins for extra texture), rinse, and keep covered in cold water until ready to add, then drain and pat dry with towel.
3. Heat a heavy-bottomed pot on medium. When hot, add enough olive oil to cover bottom. Add leeks and stir. Reduce heat to low, stirring frequently, do not allow leeks to brown.
4. When leeks are wilted, add potatoes, and continue to stir.

Keep heat low so that nothing browns.

5. Add salt and a few grinds of white pepper.

6. When potatoes are a bit tender and leeks have melted, add wine.

7. Let mixture simmer for a few minutes, then add enough broth to cover vegetables and cook until potatoes are done. Remove from heat.

8. Allow mixture to cool.

9. Add batches to food processor and blitz until mixture is smooth with a few chunky bits.

10. Taste the mixture. If it needs flavoring, add a dash of cayenne pepper and a bit more salt.

11. Return mixture to pot, and heat on low. Add as much broth as you prefer for the consistency and texture of soup you like. (The soup will continue to thicken as it heats.)

12. Serve and, if you like, sprinkle parsley on each serving.

NOTES

1. This recipe may be doubled or tripled for a crowd.

2. This soup freezes well.

HER OWN

Legacy

45

Silver spoons and forks and knives lined up like a regiment on either side of my plate. I wrapped the napkin between my fingers. My tutor never included so many tools in his etiquette lessons, lessons I wished I'd paid more attention to.

Jacques served us soup and bread. The smell of leeks and potatoes made me want to grab the tureen and gulp it all down. He poured wine into crystal goblets etched with the Verzat crest. "Anything else, Comtesse?"

Joliette flinched. "No. Merci." She might not have heard her title at all, had I not been there. She'd just met me. I was a stranger and a commoner.

Jacques left us and closed the tall double doors.

I picked up the spoon corresponding to the one Joliette took and watched how she dipped it. I doubted I could take so little, but I tried.

"You are terribly young to be a député, Monsieur." The Marquise sipped her wine. "Which section do you represent?"

The rich, savory soup coated my tongue. I swallowed. "Faubourg Saint-Antoine."

Her eyebrows lifted. "Did you rouse the peasants to attack the Bastille?"

The soup hit my empty stomach like a fist. "No."

She sniffed. "But you joined them?"

"No, I...I had to find my friend's body."

"I am so sorry for your loss." She patted her napkin about her lips. "Then I may conclude that you are not a Royalist?"

I tore off a piece of bread, so white and soft and fragrant. I wanted to chomp into the whole loaf, not think up lies. "I represent the people of Saint-Antoine, but that does not mean I am against the King, Madame. Many of my neighbors feel only the King can help them."

"In what way?" She sipped again.

"By regulating the price of bread." I held up a chunk. "By reducing taxes. By passing laws—laws that represent the poor."

"Formidable." The Marquise shivered in the blazingly hot room. "Joliette, would you be a dear and get my shawl? I left it on the dressing table."

I jumped up. "I will get it for you."

"Nonsense, you remain right where you are." The Marquise was as intimidating as Papa. Did such force come with titles?

"I will summon Marie." Joliette reached for a ribbon hanging next to the window.

"Oh, please, allow me a moment alone with this handsome young man."

I looked to Joliette, thinking: *Please don't leave me alone with her.*

The Marquise fingered the necklaces resting on her bosom. "And you should look in on the Baron."

"Very well." Joliette half smiled. "Please, continue eating. I shall be only a moment." I jumped and pulled out her chair, my heart pounding as she left us.

I sat. Should I not eat until she returned? My stomach rumbled, and I feared the Marquise heard it. I popped a piece of bread in my mouth, hoping I'd not committed a social sin.

THÉRÈSE
AND ANNE'S
MUSHROOM
SOUP

SERVES 6–8

*During the French Revolution, the practice of religion was
forbidden and a war of dechristianization was waged. The
Catholics of the Loire Valley fought back, and the rebels*

became known as Chouans, nicknamed after an owl because they imitated the bird's hoot as a warning signal during the war. Harboring Chouans or members of the clergy was a crime punishable by death. Simon discovers a Chouan family hiding in the estate's caves and the Château de Verzat becomes home to them. In this excerpt, Geneviève and Simon, both masquerading as members of the opposite sex, are on their way to Nantes.

INGREDIENTS

2 pounds of cremini mushrooms

2 pounds white button mushrooms

2 cups diced sweet onion

2 shallots finely chopped

extra virgin olive oil

12 sprigs fresh thyme

1 ½–2 quarts chicken or vegetable broth

2 tablespoons soy sauce or umami (optional)*

1 teaspoon smoked sweet paprika

1–2 cups 2% milk

2 cups nonfat Greek yogurt

sea salt and pepper

chopped fresh parsley or additional thyme

fresh lemon wedges

PROCESS

1. Thoroughly wash the mushrooms and allow them to dry on a towel. (Tip: I use new shower mitts, originally made for exfoliating, but I wear them to rub the mushrooms clean under running water. They remove all the clinging grit from the

mushrooms quickly and easily.)

2. Separate the stems from the caps and chop both into ½ inch cubes.

3. Heat a heavy-bottomed pot on low to medium. Add enough olive oil to coat the bottom and lightly sauté the mushrooms in batches with a sprinkling of fresh thyme in each. (As Julia Child is known for saying: "Don't crowd the mushrooms!") You may need to add a splash or two of oil as you continue to cook the mushrooms.

4. Remove and reserve the cooked mushrooms and their juices.

5. Add more olive oil to the pan and sauté the diced onion and shallots.

6. When onions and shallots are soft and translucent, add the cooked mushrooms, their juices, and the broth.

7. Allow to cook on low, occasionally stirring, for 20 minutes. Add soy sauce or umami if using.

8. Add paprika.

9. Add milk, stir continuously until fully incorporated.

10. Ensure the heat is at the lowest setting. Add the yogurt by tablespoonful, stirring continuously.

11. Add salt and pepper to taste.

12. Add a squeeze of lemon and chopped fresh parsley or thyme before serving.

NOTES

1. Cooks at Château de Verzat would not have had soy sauce. They would have used powdered dried mushrooms (umami)

and wine to boost the flavors of the mushrooms. If you use red wine be aware that the soup may turn a lovely shade of purple.

2.   This soup can be kept warm in a slow cooker—but keep the heat on low as the dairy in the soup will curdle and separate when the heat is high.

3.   This soup freezes well. Be sure when reheating to simmer.

HER OWN REVOLUTION

50

SIMON, SHAWL ASKEW, strained against his laced bodice as he hitched the horses to the carriage. "How do you move in these clothes, Gen?"

"Now you know why I wear breeches." Dressed in men's boots, frock coat, and cloak, I climbed up next to Simon on the driver's bench.

Hoarfrost coated the ground and barren grapevines. The cold breeze held the odor of dead leaves and a metallic scent of impending snow. I pulled Simon close and folded a blanket over our legs.

He smacked my arm. "Not taking liberties, are you?"

I laughed. "You hate wearing my gown and bonnet, but you like hiding in plain sight."

He dabbed his handkerchief at his nose, much like the affected way a woman might. "Will you trade clothes with me?"

"The only false identity papers you have are for a woman, so you have no other choice." I blew out my frustration in a sigh. "Besides, now you're getting a taste of what women must endure."

"I never thought about that." He breathed into his hands and rubbed them. "That's why my maman always wears a shawl?"

"It's also fashionable."

"Did you like the mushroom soup we had before we left?" he asked, his eyes sparking with mischief.

"What are you up to?"

He slapped his leg. "The Chouan ladies and children have been growing mushrooms in the Verzat caves that are too narrow to store wine casks."

"That's very resourceful of them."

He thumped his chest. "It was my idea, and I showed them the tunnels. But they do all the work. They sell the mushrooms, but they make them into soup for all the orphans."

"The soup was delicious."

UNCLE LOUIS'S LENTIL SOUP

SERVES 6–8

Louis LaGarde rescued Geneviève, who is wanted for having saved him and hundreds of innocents from the guillotine. Having escaped Paris, they arrive at LaGarde's former château which, Geneviève learns, he has turned into an orphanage. Geneviève is dressed as a man, and goes by the name, Jean Detré. Forty children sit at a long table in the former ballroom.

INGREDIENTS

½ cup diced parsnips

½ cup diced carrots

½ cup diced celery

½ cup diced red pepper

½ cup diced yellow pepper

2 sliced leeks, white part only

1 small onion, chopped

extra virgin olive oil

1 pound turkey sausage, sliced into bite-size pieces (optional)

1 ½–2 quarts chicken or vegetable broth

2 cups lentils, rinsed and picked over

½ cup dry white wine (optional)

4 cups chopped fresh kale or baby spinach

sea salt

pepper

dash of cayenne pepper

PROCESS

1. Wash, peel, and dice the first 6 vegetables. Allow them to dry on a towel.
2. In a large stock pot and over low to medium heat, sauté batches of first five vegetables in olive oil for about five minutes, do not brown. As they begin to soften, remove from pot, and add more vegetables. Remove all vegetables and cover to keep warm.
3. Add leeks and chopped onion to the pot with a dash of salt. Add more oil if needed and cook until they are soft, do not brown. Remove and add to the other cooked vegetables.
4. If you are using sausage, remove vegetables from pot, add a bit more olive oil, and sauté sausage slices until lightly browned.

5. Return all cooked vegetables to pot.
6. Add the broth and cook on low for about 10–15 minutes.
7. Add lentils and cook for 15 minutes, until lentils are soft but not mushy.
8. Add wine. Simmer for five minutes.
9. Add kale or spinach and more broth if needed. Cook on low until greens wilt.
10. Add cayenne pepper, salt, and pepper to taste.
11. Serve hot with crusty bread.

NOTES

1. This soup freezes well.

HER OWN REVOLUTION

36

LaGarde hunched over the table and scanned every child's face until he got to the last. He growled like a bear. "What is for dinner?"

"Uncle Louis's lentil soup!" they screamed. They pounded their silver spoons upon the tables. "We want Uncle Louis's soup. We want Uncle Louis's soup!"

LaGarde instructed the children to his right to scoot over and make room for me. He grabbed my shoulder and pushed me onto the bench, and he sat in the red chair.

Doors at the other end of the room opened, and kitchen servants brought out huge pots of steaming soup and ladled it into the porcelain bowls.

After I was served, I inhaled a rich earthy scent, and took a taste. It was delicious. I looked at LaGarde. "Why do they call this 'Uncle Louis's soup?'"

He blushed. It was the first time I had seen him blush, and I felt a tug of fondness for him. I gulped my wine.

"When the children first came here, they said the lentil soup tasted like chamber-pot slops." He laughed and leaned close to me. "They had been starving, so I thought they were probably right. The next day I went to the garden and picked things I had liked as a child: sweet carrots, nutty parsnips, tender greens. I instructed Cook to dice and sauté and add them to the lentil soup—" he dropped his voice, "I did not call it chamber-pot slops. I also poured in some wine when she was not looking." He grinned. "That evening, I told the children I added magic to the soup. They were tentative, but in the end, they licked their bowls clean. Now they call it 'Uncle Louis's soup."

I laughed with him. I wanted to stay in this place forever, a place where people made others happy, a place where everyone belonged to this family, a place where everyone felt safe. I felt safe. And it was all because of LaGarde's generosity.

SOUPER SOUP PARTY TIPS

A SOUPER WAY TO BUILD COMMUNITY

I've thrown soup parties for holidays, birthdays, anniversaries—
all kinds of celebrations.

No introductions needed. Soup Parties are a *souper* way to get
people talking to each other—at the slow cookers where they
discuss the soups and trade recommendations, like: *Don't miss the
Carrot-Ginger!*

SIMPLIFY INVITATIONS

The day after Thanksgiving, we send out a Save-the-date email,
letting our guests know when we'll be having the Soup Party,
which usually occurs on the second or third Saturday in December.

We list the Soup Menu and invite people to bring bread or
something unique to their celebration of the holidays. Our Danish
friends made Aebleskiver. Our French friends baked Madelines.
An Indian friend brought curry. An Italian friend delivered Anti-
pasti. Every year, one dear friend creates cookies just like the ones
my great aunt baked.

SERVING TIPS

Create a soup bar or table

On our soup table, I connect all the slow cookers to two power strips and hide the wires under a centerpiece. You can use a decorative napkin or placemat or a sheet of fiberfill as a stand-in for snow. One year, I robbed angels from the tree and placed them on the fiberfill. The angels appeared to be skiing down a mountain slope (of wires covered in "snow"). Use your imagination. Once we placed soups around the house, but messes were created everywhere instead of just one place.

Label the soups

If a soup contains an ingredient that guests may be allergic to, note it on the label. I have antique-looking placeholder stands, and I use little black chalk boards as well. A sturdy card folded into a V-shape is a simple and elegant solution.

Serve at least one vegan and one vegetarian soup

Make a vegan soup that can be eaten by vegetarians. Also serve soups for guests who seek gluten-free and lactose-free options.

If you serve soup with nuts, post a warning!

As My Chevalier is from Virginia, I've made peanut soup. I labeled that soup in RED and forewarned all our guests when I greeted them.

Serve soups that will survive staying warm in a slow cooker for a few hours

No cheese or cream-based soups, and no soups with pasta because the pasta will continue to cook—making glue of your soup.

Have extra broth on hand

The soups will thicken, so microwave the appropriate broth in a glass measuring cup and add small amounts throughout the evening.

Keep ladles with their soups on separate spoon rests

No contamination of vegetarian with chicken or nuts with anything else. Each soup should have its own ladle on a spoon rest in front of it.

Set up a dessert table

Most of our guests enjoy bringing desserts, so we set up a special table just for sweets in another room, which ensures guests move around. Turn wineglasses upside down and place plates atop them to create different levels so you can accommodate more dishes.

Create a nonalcoholic beverage table separate from the bar with alcohol

Especially important if you're inviting kids.

Place stacks of cocktail napkins everywhere

Helps cleanup spills and sticky fingers.

Shoot plenty of photos

And encourage your guests to send theirs to you.

Make it interactive

We ask guests to vote for their favorite soup. We print out a menu, attach it to a clipboard, add a pen, and pass it around.

Follow up with an email announcing
the Favorite Soup of the Year

Tally the votes and let guests know the winning soup of that year. Thank all the guests who brought goodies to share. Be prepared for a flurry of recipe sharing!

Enjoy the
tradition next year!

RESOURCES

A Few of My Favorite Ingredients

FLAVORED OLIVE OILS

OMG!® Herbs de Provence Olive Oil, Sundried Tomato Balsamic
Dipping Oil, and Extra Virgin Olive Oil with Meyer Lemon
available at:
OMGOLIVEOILS.COM/
COLLECTIONS/ALL-OLIVE-OILS

FRUITY WHITE BALSAMIC VINEGARS

OMG!® D'Anjou Pear White Balsamic Vinegar and Blueberry
White Balsamic Vinegar available at: https://omgoliveoils.com/
collections/all-balsamic-vinegars

ORGANIC EXTRA VIRGIN OLIVE OIL FOR ROASTING AND SAUTÉING

Costco Kirkland Signature™ Organic Extra Virgin Olive Oil

ORGANIC CHICKEN BROTH

Trader Joe's Organic Free Range Chicken Broth

ORGANIC VEGETABLE BROTH

Trader Joe's Organic Vegetable Broth

UMAMI

Trader Joe's Mushroom & Company UMAMI Seasoning Blend

CLICQUOT
INTRODUCES
THE AUTHOR

Photo by Berry Edwards

MY MOM HAS had many careers. She debuted, at the age of five, as a model at a local country club where her crinoline petticoat dropped to her ankles in the middle of the runway. Wish I had been there for that!

She's been a clothing designer, actress (starring in her first television commercial with Jeff Daniels for S.O.S. Soap Pads), TV show host, spokesperson for high-tech companies, marketing and public relations professional, and technical writer for Fortune 100 companies.

I'm proud that her work has appeared in *The New York Times*, *San Francisco Chronicle*, *The Christian Science Monitor*, and *The Writer*, among others. Her short stories have been published in anthologies and independently.

A graduate of the Fashion Institute of Technology, she weaves her knowledge of textiles and clothing design throughout her historical French fiction. She brings her passions for France, wine, and cooking to all her work. The proud owner of ten slow cookers, she is renowned for her annual Soup Parties at which she serves soups from different cultures. The parties are fun, but no one shares their soup with me—bummer.

Debra's Château de Verzat series follows headstrong and independent women and the four-hundred loyal families who protect a Loire Valley château and vineyard and its legacy of producing the finest wines in France during the French Revolution. *Soups of Château de Verzat* is her first cookbook.

She lives in the Pacific Northwest with her family and me, her standard poodle. I'm named after a fine French Champagne.

Clicquot

SPREADING THE WORD

Word of mouth is the best way to discover books, so if you'd like to help spread the word, please share your review. My mom greatly appreciates your feedback.

AMAZON.COM/AUTHOR/DEBRABORCHERT
GOODREADS.COM/DEBRA_BORCHERT

If you'd like a complimentary e-story and recipes, visit:
DEBRABORCHERT.COM

A NOTE FROM CLICQUOT

Clicquot's Pupsicles

SERVES 4

Photo by Debra Borchert

*My mom makes these in the summer for me. She usually uses kibble,
but when she wants to make me happiest, she uses treats!*

INGREDIENTS

4 tablespoons of your dog's favorite kibble or treats

2 cups chicken or beef broth

PROCESS

1. Pour the kibble and or treats in the bottom of a 1-cup plastic container. (Yogurt cups work well for this.)
2. Pour the broth over the kibble.
3. Cover and freeze for eight hours.
4. Remove from freezer when ready to serve and pop the pupsicle out of the container.
5. Sit back and enjoy your dog licking the pupsicle for the treasure!

ACKNOWLEDGEMENTS

Taste Testers

Thank you for your courage and honesty in tasting many, many soups.

Paulette Adams, Pattie Allen, Cynthia Baxter, Alice K. Boatwright, Tiffanny Brooks, Luanne Brown, Andy Chang, Chrissy Consolā of Parisian Niche, Carol Despeaux Fawcett, Berry Edwards, Bill & Jan Edwards, Conner Edwards, Lauren Edwards, Elaine Gibbs, Gyda Harris, Joanne Kuhns, Jill MacGregor, Ib Odderson, Erik Odderson, Eva Odderson, Paristoo, Susan Patten, Donna Reynolds, Ingrid Salmon, Albert Sbragia, Dorette Snover, Jane Sutherland, Jennifer White, Holly & Larry Williams.

Clicquot wishes to thank Cinamon and Lello for their participation in taste-testing her pupsicles.

BOOK
EXCERPTS

HER

OWN

LEGACY

I

Joliette
Château de Verzat, August 30, 1786

"WINE FLOWS IN your veins." Grandmaman brought her lorgnette to her eyes, examining the underside of a grape leaf.

I walked with her through the undulating hills covered in grape-vines. Bees swarmed the grapes' syrupy juices, their humming reverberating in my chest, reassuring me I was home. Ever since I could walk, I accompanied Grandmaman on her daily inspections of the vineyard. I peered over her shoulder at the leaves, but I did not see any mites or cutworms. "My tutor told me blood flows in our veins."

She nodded and brought her arm beneath the leaves, lifted them, and exposed the grapes, round and full and close to ripe. "It does. But you are a Verzat, and wine is in your blood."

"That is silly." A giggle rolled through me. "You know I am allowed only sips—I am just twelve."

"It is not from the drinking of wine." She straightened and dug the tip of her walking stick into the cracked earth, releasing a mineral scent. "It is from the terroir. Everything around you contributes to the wine and your blood."

I laughed. "You are making that up."

"I am not." She lifted her cane, waggling it at me. "You are as rooted to this estate as the vines, and I shall prove it. Close your eyes."

As always, I obeyed her.

"What do you smell?"

A trickle of sweat ran down my neck. I was grateful I was not wearing the tight sleeves or heavy underskirts required at the Court of Versailles. I wanted to give her the correct answer. To her dismay, my papa had no interest in the vineyard, and I often heard him arguing with Grandmaman about it. I could not further disappoint her. A cool breeze brought the scents of mud and fish from the Loire, but they merely influenced the terroir, they were not a part of it, like the earth that rooted the vines.

I turned my back to the wind. Another fruit, besides the grapes. I sniffed again. Peaches? I inhaled a scent so luscious, my mouth watered. "Sun-ripened apricots." I opened my eyes.

Her smile lit up her face and warmed me. She lifted her stick toward the far hill, where an orchard grew. She wobbled, and I reached to steady her until she replanted her stick. "You would not have been able to identify that scent if you did not have wine in your blood."

There was no arguing with her. "Will this year produce as good a vintage as the last?"

She adjusted my bonnet to shade my face. "You have your maman's luminous complexion, and we must protect it, else she will forbid your accompanying me." She pinched my chin. "What else do you smell, child?"

Another scent? My tutor gave fewer tests. I inhaled deeply. A thick aroma shimmered in the heat, as if I had entered a patisserie. "A sweet nectar, like honey."

Her face glowed. "The fruit is smaller globed than most years but bursting with ripeness. Look." She ran a finger along strands of juice trickling from a split grape. "Aging will intensify the ambrosial flavor that accompanies that scent." Her blue eyes sparkled, casting magic, as she searched the vineyard, stopping when she spotted a tall man. "Joseph!" She waved her cane.

Wearing a dilapidated straw hat and blue tunic, Joseph waved and loped through the vines to us. He removed his hat and bowed. "Yes, Madame la Comtesse?"

"Send the pickers here this afternoon."

"Just the southern slope, Madame?"

Her smile broadened. "This is why you are an excellent vigneron, Joseph. You require specifics. Yes, just the southern slope. Will you join us on our walk?"

"Of course, Madame." Joseph followed us at a respectful distance.

"You will see why I am grooming Joseph as my apprentice until you can take over, my dear." Grandmaman cupped her fingers along my cheek, and I leaned into her touch like a puppy nuzzling its maman.

"That will not be for a long time. I have much to learn."

She tapped the tip of my nose. "You have a vintner's sense of smell. That honeylike scent makes the wine robust and gives some wines a hint of caramel, like the caramel in Cook's pastries. It only occurs during years of scant rainfall. I believe this year will be an excellent vintage, better than the last."

I picked a grape and savored the taste, imagining how the flavor would change after fermentation. The cracked dry soil released puffs of chalky dust with our footsteps. If I breathed through my mouth, I tasted the chalk. Like the parched earth, I wanted to soak up every drop of her knowledge. "But if there is little rainfall, will the harvest yield less fruit?"

She planted her walking stick and lifted her face to the sun, her wrinkles slipping away in the golden light. "You are correct. And you have the mind of a viticulturist." She tilted her head, examining me.

I wrapped my tongue around the word, forming it silently and feeling a strange pride growing in me for having the mind of an expert.

"Rather a large word for the growing of grapes. True?" Her lips formed a pink heart. The black lace cascading over her straw bonnet and tied beneath her chin accentuated the heart shape. Leaning on her cane, she wavered a bit.

"Viticulture?"

"Oh, how I wish your father had been as curious at your age. He has the Verzat palate, of course." She stabbed the earth with her walking stick. "But he did not, and still does not, possess the desire for learning how to preserve the Verzat legacy."

A tightness wrapped around my chest—pressing me to not disappoint her. Yet, out of loyalty, I hastened to defend my father. "Papa granted the vassals houses and land on the estate in return for their working the vineyard."

"Yes. That was democratic of him, and he is a good businessman." She twisted her stick in the dirt. "Your father considers himself a student of the Enlightenment. He spent many years studying Locke and Rousseau."

I turned and pretended to examine a leaf. He had encouraged me to read the same, but I did not confess it.

"In recent years he spent much time with that American…the man with the funny fur hat…what is his name?"

I laughed. "Monsieur Benjamin Franklin. He made embarrassing mistakes in French, and Papa had difficulties not laughing at the Ambassador's faux pas."

"That is the man. My son is more interested in the American democracy than the Verzat winery. But should Château de Verzat fail, the land will be sold. And four hundred families will either go back to being vassals or be without homes and work. And it would be the end of the Verzat legacy."

A niggling sensation moved through my stomach. "It will not fail so long as you run the winery, Grandmaman."

"For now. I am nearly sixty and will not be here forever to ensure its success." Her eyes grew moist.

I squinted in the bright light. She could not leave me. I would die without her. I reached out and held her arm. "You are too young to die, Grandmaman."

OR VISIT:

AMAZON.COM/HER-LEGACY-CH%C3%
A2TEAU-VERZAT-BOOK-EBOOK/DP/B0B9HWDMFH

HER
OWN
REVOLUTION

I

Paris
August 3, 1793

I<small>F</small> I <small>HAD</small> the same rights as a man, I would not have to dress as one.

After waiting for Cook to leave for the market, I raced through the kitchen, down the servants' stairs, and into the cellar. The pungent odors of ripe apples, stale wine, and fusty onions thickened the air. I pulled out my bundle from behind the vinegar cask and unbuttoned my gown.

The irony of having to masquerade as a man to have equal rights made me want to spit in Robespierre's face. I wrapped a strip of cloth tightly around my breasts. All the talk of Liberté, Egalité, Fraternité. I pulled on my brother's tunic.

Liberty? All women were free to do was starve. I stepped into my brother's breeches and knotted a ribbon at my waist.

Equality? Pah! Our latest government passed a law enabling all men to vote. I tied my neckcloth.

Brotherhood? What about sisterhood? I shoved my arms into the waistcoat. After four years of governmental discussion, girls were finally guaranteed an elementary education. But universities were still closed to women.

Voices from the kitchen stilled me. If my stepmother caught me, she'd send me to a nunnery. My fingers grew numb from grasping the frock coat lapels. Her heavy footsteps headed for the dining room. I shook out my stiff hands.

We had won the right to divorce, but how were all the divorced women supposed to support their children? The memory of Lisette, my former neighbor, standing amongst the prostitutes gathered at the banks of the Seine, calling and taunting sailors, chilled me.

I stomped my feet into the too-big boots. An unmarried woman's signature was still worthless. But not in America—there women could own businesses and property. I should have gone to America with Henri. I should not have been so stubborn. I had been his mistress for a year, why had I refused to accompany him as one? I adjusted the breeches, trying to ignore my own nagging voice: He never said, I love you.

Coiling my hair into a bun, I pushed my brother's tricorne down over my curls, opened the cellar door, and peeked out into the late afternoon. A steady rain beat upon the cobbles, washing chamber-pot slops into the gutter at the street's center. The heels of my brother's boots were higher than my usual shoes, and I concentrated on keeping my balance as I straddled the gutter.

Staying on narrow back streets, I adjusted my gait, trying to appear confident. As was my habit, I began to pick up my skirts but clutched the frock coat instead and looked around for anyone who might have seen me.

If caught impersonating a man, any other woman would appear before the Public Prosecutor—my father—who would order her head shaved and sentence her to an insane asylum. But if I were arrested, I would disappoint my father, who would feel obligated to make an example of me. As he had recently sentenced Charlotte Corday, the first woman to be guillotined, I feared being dragged before him far more than eight-months in a madhouse.

I splashed through puddles. If I didn't sail for America soon, my stepmother would have me married to an old goat I didn't love. But if I had identity papers proving I was a man, I could get a job that paid enough money for passage. Henri had urged me to visit his printer friend, Pierre. How would I convince Pierre to make false papers—a traitorous crime, for him and me? What if Pierre refused, or worse, told my father? I'd make Pierre agree. Today.

Dark gray clouds hung over the river and twisted up the turrets of la Conciergerie, the new home to Marie Antoinette. Even if Henri couldn't marry me, I was going to join him in America, no matter what crimes I had to commit. Surely he'd tell me he loved me when he saw me again.

Rain slid down the back of my neck, making me shiver. I pulled up my collar. The only right women earned that was equal to a man's was the privilege of facing Madame Guillotine.

OR VISIT
AMAZON.COM/HER-OWN-REVOLUTION-CH%C3%A2TEAU-VER-
ZAT-EBOOK/DP/B0BYKFQGLG

HER
OWN

AR

I

Geneviève
Loire Valley, France
August 1797

A RAINSTORM COULD HARM the harvest; hail would ruin it. Across the still Loire River dark clouds mushroomed above workers reaping hayfields. Weeks of hot weather had ripened a bountiful grape crop, and all four hundred families who lived on the estate were in the vineyard furiously picking.

I reached beneath the leaves, clipping grape clusters and placing them in a large basket. Removing my straw bonnet, I wiped sweat from my brow and rubbed my lower back. Could this ache be a sign I was with child? Although it was too early to tell, a thread of hope ran through me.

A few feet away, Aurélia clipped a bunch of grapes and smiled at me, her round black eyes offering sympathy. Tall and slim, she moved with the grace of a poplar bending with a breeze. She pulled a fan from her hanging pocket and offered it.

"Thank you." I waved it, savoring the stirring air. A finely hand-painted scene on delicate silk depicted the Seine. "This is Paris. I hope when we are not at war, we can visit the city together." I closed it and held it out, but she put up her palm.

Wearing a simple blue day gown and long white apron, she had the regal bearing of a queen. She mouthed, *You need it more than I.*

I understood Aurélia, without her voice, although I would love to hear her speak if she regained her ability. I tucked the fan into my belt and smiled at my past foolishness—I had feared I could never be friends with my former-lover's wife. Aurélia was more than a friend; she was the sister I had always wanted.

Down the hill, a distant spot of color caught my eye. Two officers on horseback trotted along the river road, their red frock coats flaring against the gray clouds.

"The last officers conscripted four of our fine men, and they all died on the battlefield." I wiped my sticky hands on my apron. "I'll not let them take even one more of our men to waste in their war." Every man of conscription age had to hide, and my husband knew all of them. I searched the vineyard and spied him. "Louis!"

He stopped the team of horses pulling a wagon laden with grapes.

I pointed at the two soldiers.

He handed the reins to a worker and ran, shouting through the fields. Young men darted around vines toward the cave. The officers would die of starvation before they found them in the network of Verzat caves.

The sky darkened. "Aurélia, the storm is coming. Best take the children back to the château."

She mouthed, *The rain will be cooling.*

"But it might hail."

She mouthed, *We will be fine.*

I hoped she was right. My four-year-old stepdaughter sat on the dry, cracked earth holding a basket nearly as big as she was and waving her hand. "Tante Gen, why are there so many wasps?"

I swiped at a lock of hair stuck to my cheek. Louis and I had been married a year and still Louisa called me *aunt*.

Aurélia's three-year-old son sat on the ground next to Louisa, holding another basket. As she clipped clusters, Aurélia gently toyed with the vines, making the leaves tickle Charles. He threw back his head and laughed.

"Why are there so many wasps?" Louisa asked again.

"They like the sweet juice," I replied.

A low rumble stopped my picking. The advancing clouds darkened to the color of charcoal. "I pray the clouds empty themselves before they cross the river." The officers turned their horses and headed east, toward Tours. My shoulders relaxed as I resumed clipping. But a stirring in my stomach nagged me. Old people and children were in the vineyards. Should I order everyone to seek shelter now in case of hail? The workers were so loyal, I doubted they would leave their work.

Louisa screeched and kicked her foot at a wasp. "I want to go home, now."

Lightning flickered over the hayfield. A louder rumble followed. Everyone else continued their work. I dared not leave. I waved my apron over her. "I won't let them hurt you."

Charles reached out. "Take my hand, Louisa. I'm not afraid."

"You are very brave, Charles," I said.

Louisa grabbed his hand. "I'm brave, too."

Cold air dropped over us like a curtain. Lightning brightened the sky. Gooseflesh ran up my arms. A sharp odor, like scorched metal, sliced the air. Had lightning struck a wagon? Workers in the hayfield flung their scythes away from them and threw themselves flat upon the ground, covering their heads with their arms. I should order our workers to take shelter. I turned to run to the alarm bell.

The sound of a roaring river charged toward us.

Louisa screamed and covered her ears. I swept her up and brought her to my chest.

Lightning lashed across the sky like a whip. A deafening crash followed.

Torrents of rain poured down like we were standing under a waterfall. I bent over, protecting Louisa, and the force of water pushed the breath from me.

We dared not run for cover. Lightning sought the highest target, and should we run, we would be it.

The rain lessened. Pinging and clacking sounds seized my breath. "Hail," I shouted. "Aurélia. Cover Charles with your basket."

Pebbles of ice the size of pearls popped and bounced on the crusty earth.

"Papa!" Louisa cried. "I want Papa."

I grabbed her basket and dumped the grapes on the ground. Falling to my knees, I pushed Louisa down.

Aurélia slapped the ground under the vines.

"Good idea." I pulled Louisa under the vines for shelter. "Curl up on your side, like a puppy." She whined and fought me as I wrangled her under the basket. "Hush, you will be safe, but you must stay covered."

Aurélia brought Charles next to Louisa and put her basket over him. Louisa's hand crept out from under the wicker and searched for Charles. His fingers gripped hers.

Thunder boomed so loudly my teeth chattered.

With the children between us, Aurélia and I joined arms and pressed ourselves over the baskets. "Keep your head down and your bonnet covering your face."

Hail broke off chunks of my straw hat. Leaves and vines whirled past. Hailstones floated atop sheets of rainwater that slicked the impenetrable ground, pushing the pellets against the vine roots and piling up the hail like snowbanks. A shard of ice stung my cheek. I wiped the burn, and blood stained my fingers. I longed to shout at the workers to take cover.

Louisa screeched and kicked the basket, knocking it off her. I lunged, pulled the basket back over her.

"I want Papa!" She kicked a hole in the basket and thrust out her foot. I pushed it back.

Charles shouted, "Don't cry, Louisa. I'm here."

Ice chunks, now as large as plums, pounded us, crashed over us like a rockslide.

Punishing hailstones bruised my back. A strange clacking noise surrounded us. Hailstones clattered atop piles of icy pellets. Blood dripped onto my skirts.

Gusting wind ripping vines from the posts sounded like tearing cloth.

I prayed Louis and the pickers had taken cover under the wagon. Please, don't let it get worse. Don't let the hail destroy everything. Please let no one be injured.

Lightning cracked. I counted to three before thunder boomed again. The storm was moving east of us—away from the vineyard, not deeper into it. My grip on the basket eased. Please let everyone be safe.

The rumbling and crashing stopped as suddenly as it began. The wind calmed. Rain pattered. Ceased. Hailstones bobbed in rainwater, mixed with the dust, and sluiced around us in chalky streams. A bank of ice surrounded my legs, making me shiver.

Strong sunlight beat upon my back. I straightened, squinting in the brilliant light. Where was Louis?

Broken shoots dangled from vines. Splintered canes stabbed the earth. Battered leaves and smashed grape clusters littered the vineyard. A blackbird lay squawking, fluttering its crippled wing.

We were ruined.

OR VISIT
AMAZON.COM/GP/PRODUCT/B0B9KN1536

THE VINEYARD AND CHÂTEAU THAT INSPIRED CHÂTEAU DE VERZAT

WHILE RESEARCHING IN France's Loire Valley, I discovered Château Brézé, an historical monument surrounded by a vineyard not far from Saumur. The BBC filmed a wonderful video, "The Medieval 'Doomsday Bunker' Hidden Beneath a Castle," walking viewers through the deep network of tunnels under the château that forms one of Europe's largest underground fortresses. Video by Mathieu Orcel and Augustin Muniz.

View it here:

DEBRABORCHERT.COM